Help for Rosie

BY MICHÈLE DUFRESNE

Pioneer Valley Educational Press, Inc.

"Help!" cried Rosie.
"Help!"

Bella ran to Rosie.
"What's the matter, Rosie?"
asked Bella.

Rosie started to shake.
"Mom is taking me to the vet for a shot!"

"A shot!" said Bella.
"Oh, no!
Is she taking me, too?"

Rosie shook her head.
"No," she said. "Just me!"

"Come on," said Bella.
"You can hide."
Bella ran up the stairs.
"Come on and hide upstairs,"
she called.

Rosie looked up at Bella.
"I can't go up the stairs," said Rosie.
"I'm afraid of the stairs!"

Bella ran to the couch. She crawled under the couch and looked up at Rosie. "Come on! You can hide under here," she said.

"That won't work," said Rosie. "Mom will see me!"

"I have an idea," said Rosie. "You can pretend to be me! You can put on my sweater!" She pushed her pink sweater to Bella.

"Oh, no! Forget that idea," said Bella and she pushed the sweater back to Rosie.

"**Ohhhh, no!**" said Bella.
"Forget that idea!"